Piggy Pie Po

3 Little Stories

Written by Audrey Wood

Pictures drawn by Audrey Wood and painted by Don Wood

Harcourt Children's Books

Houghton Mifflin Harcourt

Boston New York 2010

Harcourt Children's Books is an imprint of
Houghton Mifflin Harcourt Publishing Company.

www.hmhbooks.com

The illustrations in this book were painted with acrylics on canvas.
The text type was set in Raleigh.
The display type was set in OPTI Cloister.
Designed by Regina Roff.

Library of Congress Cataloging-in-Publication Data is available.
LCCN: 2009941275
ISBN 978-0-15-202494-9

Manufactured in Singapore
TWP 10 9 8 7 6 5 4 3 2 1
4500220980

For Nikah P. De Vito

Piggy Pie Po likes to dance

when he wears his party pants.

If he wears his rubber fins,

Piggy Pie Po swims and swims.

When he wears his yellow coat,

Piggy Pie Po likes to boat.

If he wears his working shirt,

he'll be digging in the dirt.

But when he's ready for the tub,
to splish and splash and rub-a-dub,
Piggy Pie Po wears no clothes . . .

only bubbles, head to toes.

Piggy Pie Po is so smart,

he can do the finest art.

He can beat upon his drum

while counting backwards, ten to one.

Every book upon his shelf

he can read all by himself.

For a penny he will spell
pistachio and *pimpernel.*

But there's one thing he can't do . . .

Piggy Pie can't tie his shoe — yet!

No one was home at half-past nine

when Piggy Pie Po came to dine.

He ate a peach.

He ate some plums.

The lemon pie is only crumbs!

He spilled the soup!
He didn't care.

He got it in his piggy hair.

He tromped upon the yummy cake.

Then he made a

BIG

mistake!

He ate a pepper.

So hot!

So red!

He ran straight home . . .
and went to bed.